Flanimals of the Deep

by
Ricky Gervais

Illustrated by
Rob Steen

ff

First published in 2006
by Faber and Faber Limited
3 Queen Square London WC1N 3AU

This edition published in 2007

Manufactured in China by Imago

A CIP record for this book
is available from the British Library

ISBN 978–0–571–23404–2

2 4 6 8 10 9 7 5 3 1

Contents

You really don't need to know anything else about Flanimals, in fact you never did. I was lying before.

Chapter 1

In the Beginning

In the beginning there was nothing. Then there was some more, and soon there was quite a lot. There was the universe, the stars, and around the stars were planets, and some of the planets had sky and land and sea and stuff.

I can't believe I haven't told you this before but Flanimal
life only exists on one planet. But that is more than enough,
trust me. I say trust me because some people make stuff up
and they are not to be trusted. In fact, most people make
stuff up now and again, so I want you to trust me because
this is all true. The problem is people who make stuff up and
shouldn't be trusted always say "trust me". So I don't know
who to believe. At least I'm honest. Or am I? Who knows?
I do obviously.

Anyway, all life started in water. Things start better wet. I don't make the rules. The first Flanimal life form, as you know, was Splorn. But there are many types. The very first was Mulgi, a sort of cross between mud and light that sat on the bottom of the sea. Some were washed onto land and these evolved into all the land Flanimals. You know all about them. But most Splorn stayed in the water as Mulgi. Then Mulgi begat Krudge, which was also a cross between mud and light, but with slightly more light. Because it was lighter it sort of floated about the Mulgi. It was a little smug about this if you ask me.

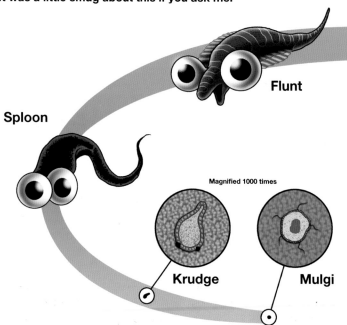

Flunt

Sploon

Magnified 1000 times

Krudge

Mulgi

Figure A. Evolution of Mulgi to Bif Uddler

Krudge evolved bi-goggles at one end and flajisplays at the other, eventually branching out as Widdles and Scrundlers. Some Krudge went the other way, developing a uniflap and becoming Sploon. Sploon grew into Flunts, and Widdles became Wumpfs. Flunts evolved upward through Iggles to Bif Uddlers as Wumpfs became Spluffs.

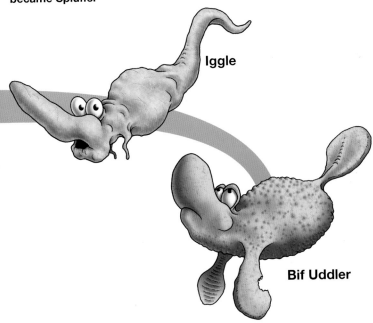

Iggle

Bif Uddler

Iggles and Uddlers are both examples of Fleptiles. They are direct descendants of the prehistoric Slubberdon. Despite millions of years of evolution the Iggles hardly changed. Then all of a sudden some evolved into Bif Uddlers in a few weeks. This was probably too soon and some of them are still not used to it. Tough! Live with it.

Widdles and Scrundlers are both examples of Multiprods. The Widdle is a woctomble (eight wormbloiders), while the Scrundler is a wextomble (six wormbloiders). The Widdle has an extended gogstalk for surface snogling in the shallows. It widdles its wormbloiders to attract Sea Flugs — its main prey. The Scrundler is a bottom feeder. It feeds off the bottoms of other Flanimals. Widdling would aggravate the situation. Scrundling keeps it fair.

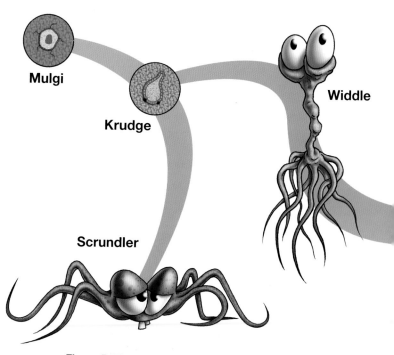

Figure B. Evolution of Mulgi to Spluff and Scrundler

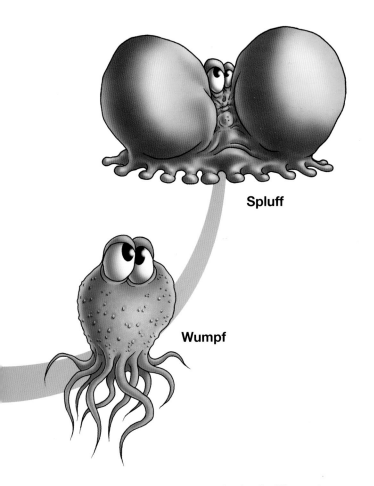

Spluff

Wumpf

Flanimal evolution happened over hundreds of millions of years then slowed down a bit. Some of the Flanimals were fed up with the fact that they weren't getting enough credit for these changes.

A strange story went around that Flanimals hadn't evolved but were made in no time at all by one creature named Grob, who no one had ever seen but was everywhere. Yes, it doesn't make any sense does it?

Grob

Only the most primitive and stupid Flanimals believed this. The clever ones knew that such a creature was impossible. You have seen how diverse the Flanimal kingdom is, how amazing life on the planet is. How could anyone create all this by design, by themselves? Who could have such an imagination? They wouldn't just have to be an artist and scientific genius, why, they would have to be god-like. They would deserve to be worshipped. You'd have to buy their book at least. But no, there is only one explanation for it. All life slowly evolved and changed over billions of years.

Marvel at even more weird and wonderful life, as we take a journey to discover the truly strange Flanimals of the Deep.

Chapter 2

The Diversity of Life

Mulon

(Molo Flapian)

The Mulon is the most intelligent being on the planet.
Although it is air-breathing it has completely adapted to ocean
life and successfully dominated the planet. It has done this not
by changing the nature of its world to fit its needs, but rather by
evolving and developing its own habits and needs to fit in with
nature. It believes that all life is precious and never knowingly
hurts another Flanimal. The saddest sound in the universe is the
harmonious whimper of a thousand Mulons when one dies.

Groy
(Eltopus Funtloid)

Bub squindler of epic proportions.
Too much in my opinion. Not necessary.
Silly. Am I wrong? Am I overreacting?
No, I don't think so.

Sleeb

(Muttinus Rump)

Sleeb are glumflorary hogglers.
They snuffle around slowly for a few
months then rest.

Molf
(Snargantua)

The Molf or Sea Drog is a killing machine. It swims and eats, that's all it does. Well, it kills as well, but that's more of a by-product of eating. It has to eat, and it has to swim to catch something to eat. That's the two main things it does, but obviously if you tear something to shreds to swallow it, it tends to die. All I'm saying is the killing is pretty much covered by the eating part. If I said my friend was ripped to pieces and eaten by a Molf, you wouldn't say

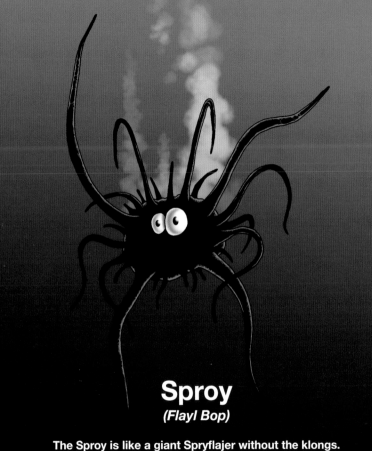

Sproy
(Flayl Bop)

The Sproy is like a giant Spryflajer without the klongs.
It more than makes up for the lack of klongs with its over-
developed noizels. It uses these to froob and nung about
viciously. If you were to meet one and it started doing
this it would take about eight seconds before you would shout

Plumph
(Pustulous Skragling)

The Plumph can suck its eyes into its
habdolible mash sack for protection. This is not its only
protection. On its outer skin it has a corrosive acid sloop.
Unfortunately when it folds its eyes in and they come into
contact with this sloop it blinds itself painfully.
IDIOT!

Hungloid
(Osifus Habilet)

If this scraley mung-trout were to
ask you "Am I ugly?" what would you say?
Would you tell the truth? You should always
tell the truth. Go on, tell the truth,
he knows anyway.

Klug Snipe
(Elm Snaggling)

This fuggling probe wangler is revolting.
Inside it is full of love and only wants to do good.
But look at it, it's revolting.

Roxstrambler
(Grimpus Slumpecker)

This encrunted shlog pike is wrong.
I don't know how it happened and it is keeping
schtum. No one is happy about this but there is
nothing anyone can do. It's here.

Spryflajer
(Crackoid Mentis)

This sploonatic junk munker is flapped out.
It plashes and streds to confuse its prey. Just when they think
they cannot be confused any more the Flajer swims away
without eating them, leaving them totally mind-spryed. Pointless.

Splug
(Gastlypodus Lumpi)

This flob of panflange would annoy me if it wasn't
for the fact that it hates itself more than I ever could.
In a way, I'm torn. Do I want it squashed so I don't have to
look at its revolting mugsluvage? Or do I want it to carry
on living because that's the thing that hurts it most?

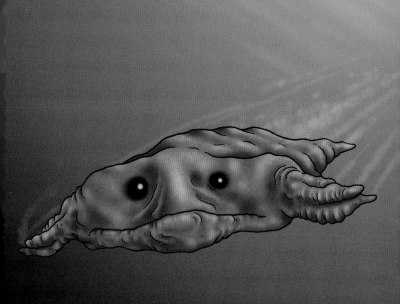

Blamp
(Credipus Slunk)

Ah, look at the Blamp. Look at his sad face.
He is slow and old. They are all slow and old, even the
young ones. They are lonely and bored. But you can't
not like them, it's actually against the law.

Ungler Water Mungler

(Gruntloidian Mampaddler)

This brontial mamb sludger is related to the Mung Ungler
but is even bigger, more sluggish and wishes for death more
regularly. It has evolved for ocean life by swapping legs for splash
flaps and growing its rear milky sea puddings into humungous
float baps. The bad news is this makes it turn upside down in
the water. The good news is it drowns and is put out of
its suckling misery.

The Lazabranks

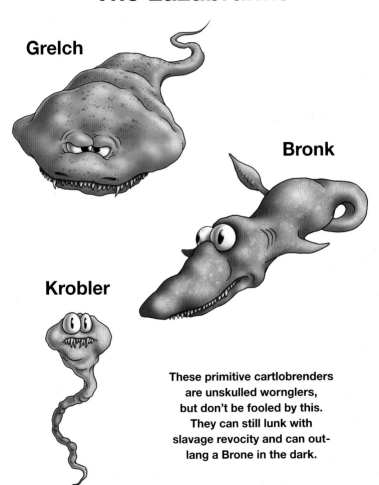

Grelch

Bronk

Krobler

These primitive cartlobrenders
are unskulled wornglers,
but don't be fooled by this.
They can still lunk with
slavage revocity and can out-
lang a Brone in the dark.

The Skellyosts

The Skellyosts are the floaty ribblers of the sea. They are extremely diverse but all have one thing in common — they are freakingly ugly. They live alone. They do this from choice because they don't want to be seen with all the other ugly freaks, not realising that they themselves are just as stomach-churningly revolting. Luckily they have no stomach to churn. The Skellyosts include Snish, Scrownocks, Brones and Skrolls.

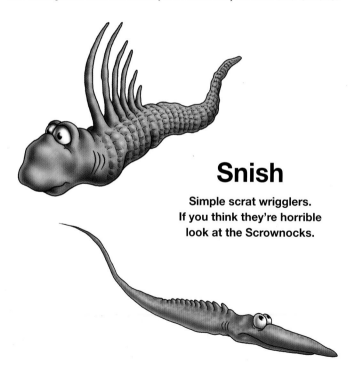

Snish

Simple scrat wrigglers.
If you think they're horrible
look at the Scrownocks.

Scrownocks

These goggle scretchers make a hideous
spine-tingling scream. Oh no, it gets worse,
look at the Brones.

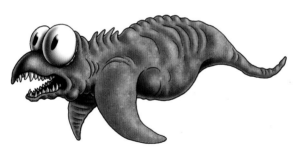

Brones

Nashy snappers that don't look so
bad when you consider the Skrolls.
Just look at them.

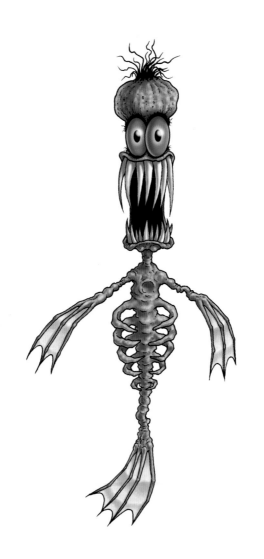

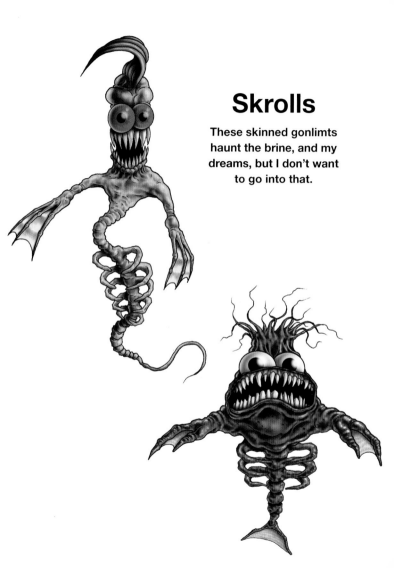

Skrolls

These skinned gonlimts haunt the brine, and my dreams, but I don't want to go into that.

Flantation

Weedles

Flantation is nowhere as diverse as in the ocean. Weedles, Clumbs, Splungi and Flambols are just some examples of seaweebs. The Flants and the Flanimals make up the two kingdoms of life, and they have many things in common. They are both cellular structures that grow and eventually die. They both reproduce, use energy, need water and chemicals from the atmosphere, and react to their surroundings. The big difference is that Flanimals usually get their energy and nutrients from the food they eat, whereas Flants get theirs from light, and the mud and water that surround them.

They don't need to hunt so they really shouldn't have eyes. It's weird. It's not as if they can use them to see predators and flee. They can't move. All they use their eyes for is to see the thing that's going to eat them. Pathetic.

Clumbs
and Splungi

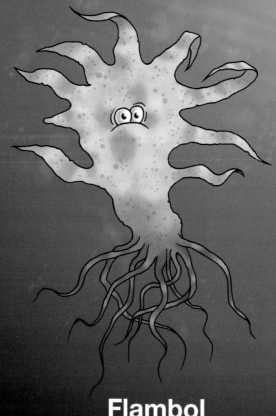

Flambol
(Flap Clabbage)

The Flambols are nothing more than floating shapes.
They have no depth. I don't just mean they're flat, I mean they
are shallow, self-centred vegetables with no personality.
I'm surprised I've found this much to say about them.

Chapter 3

The Flanisaurs

The planet was a very different place hundreds of millions of years ago. The Flanimals back then were not like the ones today. No, back then they were weird. Especially the big mental ones — the Flanisaurs.

The Grundit shares common ancestry with the Ung Noglet, but fossil evidence shows that it didn't just become the Grundit overnight. It did loads of stuff before that. It went into the sea, changed a bit, came out again, changed a bit more (in my opinion the whole sea thing was a waste of time) . . . only then did it start getting the hang of the whole Grundit vibe. Below you can see the gradual change from Slungulent Flidge through Fump Ploader and Grump Drongo to modern-day Grundit.

200 million years ago   **100 million years ago**

Evolution of
the Grundit

50 million years ago

Last Tuesday

Evolution of the
Clunge Ambler

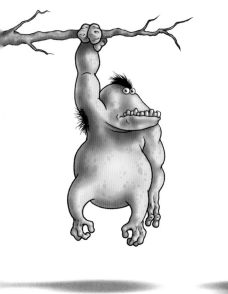

200 million years ago   100 million years ago

As you know, the Clunge Ambler is distantly related to Austrillo Ployb, but fossil evidence has again shown that some Ploybs went up into the trees and that there were many stages before they came back down to become the Clunge we know today. From primitive Chump Swangers who descended from the trees as Lum Hunchers, relying less on their arms and more on their legs, Clunge Amblers developed even more useless arms. If they carry on going the same way, in the future the Munglerone will have such useless little limbs that it won't be able to feed itself. And let me promise you this . . . no one else will feed it. No one.

Today

10 million years in the future

There were even Flanisaurs that could fly, like the Flubberdunkling, the Dilk and the Squabbler.

Flubberdunkling

These Flanisaurs evolved the means of flight over many millions of years, but they stopped flying as it became too much of a pain. Being too fat, with rubbish wings, meant some had to try so hard to stay in the air that they would literally burst.

Dilk   Squabbler

Chapter 4

The Mulons

Fossil evidence shows that Mulons evolved on land. About two hundred million years ago a strain of Blunging called Plugons roamed the planet. They were hambloid, scarbulatory creatures who would rush into the sea to escape from predators such as the Skrakalor, a Flanisaur ancestor of the Mernimbler.

In the sea too they were potential prey to fierce creatures. They had to use their superior brains to survive. They had no natural defences, no shell, no claws or fangs. They used intelligence to outwit predators. Soon, as they survived and flourished, they became lords of the deep and the most intelligent, thoughtful and creative Flanimals on the planet.

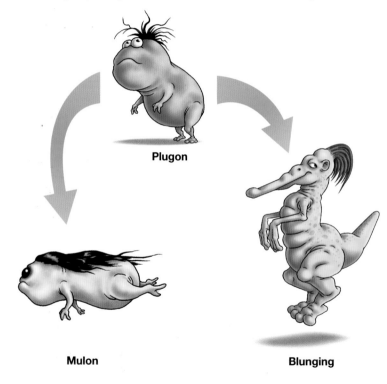

Plugon

Mulon

Blunging

Some Plugons became Mulons, some became Blungings

The problem is that being this way can be a bit boring. Soon they got a bit fed up with living underwater all the time. They would come to the shore and watch the goings-on on land. They'd been in the water so long that now they could never live on land, but they could not remember why they ever left it. They longed to see what it was like to walk, run and hop. But they never would. They were sad and started to envy the land Flanimals a bit. They weren't a jealous species, just a little sad.

Figure A. Not a chance   Figure B. Much better

Mulons live in social groups. They do this as there is safety in numbers. If you are in the middle of a big herd and a hungry Molf or Roxstrambler is hunting, you have a better chance of survival because there are hundreds of others surrounding you that can be eaten instead. It makes it a little less scary, because the sea is very scary.

It's frightening enough on land with danger around every corner. In the sea there aren't even corners – the danger is right in front of you all the time. When you are scared on land you feel short of breath. In the sea you're already short of breath so breathing is not a good idea.

Puddloflaj learning about breathing

Mulons are fascinated by life on land. Sometimes they don't believe their eyes. Their eyes had lied to them before, so once bitten, twice shy. That's the trouble with liars — you never know when to believe them. If you don't know they're liars, then you don't consider when to believe them, you just believe them. It's like the Groy who cried Molf.

Once upon a time, long, long ago (quarter past two, 6th of February, 1622), a young Groy was tending the Sleeb.

All the other Groy were busy hunting, foraging, sumping the wef, and generally doing stuff. They had left the young Groy alone with the sole responsibility of watching out for hungry Molves. If he saw an approaching Molf he was to shout "Molf! Molf!" and all the other Groy would come to defend their Sleeb. But sitting there alone watching the Sleeb he got bored. Sleeb are very boring. In fact if you start to count them you fall asleep. Sometimes you don't even need to count them. If someone were to just tell you how many there are you'd fall asleep. Even now you should be careful. Just thinking about how many Sleeb there may have been you'll start feeling a bit disinterested. Think of the Molf! Good, you're paying attention.

He sat there, bored, feeling he had been given a rubbish job to do. He wanted to have fun. Then he had an idea. A brilliant, bad, exciting idea.

"If there was a Molf, I'd shout 'Molf' and the other Groy would come swimming as fast as they could," he thought. "But the thing is, if I shouted 'Molf' and there wasn't a Molf, they'd still come swimming just as fast." So that's what he did.

"Molf! Molf!" he shouted.

"Molf! Molf!" at the top of his gills.

And sure enough, all the Groy came swimming as fast as they could.

"Where's the Molf? Where? Where?" they all gasped, wide-eyed, panicked and exhausted from their speedy swim.

There was no Molf.

All the Groy were furious.

"Don't do that again," they warned the naughty Groy. "Only shout 'Molf' when there really is a Molf and we will come swimming as fast as we can to save our Sleeb."

"OK," promised the Groy.

The next day the young Groy was watching over the flock of Sleeb and again he was bored. He just sat around doing nothing, which is dangerous because there is a Lazabrank called a Drevil that can detect a lack of movement from miles away. The less you move the quicker it finds you. It doesn't eat you it just makes you do stuff. This is very annoying if you're lazy, but the Drevil makes work for idle Flans.

Drevil

So anyway, the young Groy had another idea. I say another idea – it was exactly the same as the idea he'd had the day before. It was the same idea twice basically. The idea, in case you haven't guessed, was to shout "Molf" and see all the other Groy come swimming as fast as they could. So that's what he did.

"Molf! Molf!" he shouted. "Molf! Molf!" The other Groy came swimming as fast as they could.

"Where's the Molf?" they asked the Groy, who was very pleased his pointless plan had worked.

"Good question. There's no Molf," the naughty Groy replied.

"But you promised you wouldn't shout 'Molf' when there was no Molf," one of the other Groy pointed out.

"True. But that made the lie more believable in a way," he answered honestly.

He was honest sometimes, give him that. Even if he was being honest about lying. Be fair, come on.

The other Groy were furious . . . which is weird. They came swimming as fast as they could for fear that their Sleeb were being eaten. When they find out this is not the case they're angry. You'd think they'd be happy. The mischievous Groy was very pleased with himself.

"How funny was that?" he thought to himself. "All the other Groy came swimming as fast as they could for nothing and all the Sleeb are fine, so there was no harm done. No bad can come from a practical joke like that because I was only pretending that something awful was happening."

Just as he was thinking this he saw a terrifying sight. A huge, hungry Molf was approaching. "But not to worry," he thought. "I'll just shout 'Molf' and all the other Groy will come swimming as fast as they can."

"Molf! Molf!" he shouted. "Molf! Molf!" he shouted again. But the other Groy didn't come this time. They just assumed he was lying because of the times he had shouted "Molf" as a joke. The Molf ripped through the Sleeb, killing and eating them all, and then it swam away.

At the end of the day all the Groy returned.

"Where are all the Sleeb?" they asked.

"A Molf came and I cried 'Molf' as loud as I could, but you never came and so the Molf killed and ate all the Sleeb. Why didn't you come when I shouted 'Molf'?"

"We didn't believe you because of your stupid pranks. And now we have lost all our Sleeb. Have you learned your lesson?" said the angry mob.

"Not really," said the little Groy. "They were your Sleeb. I haven't lost anything. I'm not really bothered either way."

All the Groy were stunned.

"He's right. We're idiots."

So the moral of this tale is, of course, no matter how much a Groy lies about a Molf, always believe them when Sleeb are involved.

Anyway, where were we? Oh yes, the Mulons watching things that happen on land. There's one thing they don't like watching, and that's "The Day of the Bletchling". Once every thousand years, the millions and millions of Bletchling eggs buried deep in the ground hatch. The adult Bletchling is the most terrifying Flanimal that has ever existed. Turn to the last page if you're not afraid to see one.

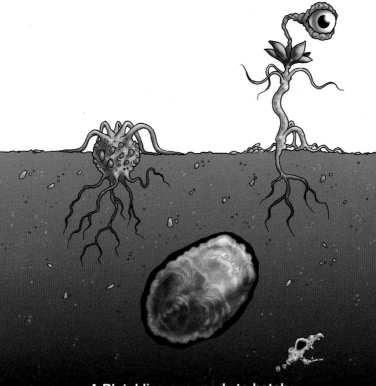

A Bletchling egg ready to hatch

Flanimal Scale Chart

Human

Bif Uddler

Blamp

Brone

Bronk

Drevil

Flambol

Grelch

Groy

Hungloid

Klug Snipe

Krobler

Molf

Mulon

Plumph

Roxstrambler

Scrownock

Skroll

Sleeb

Snish

Spluff

Splug

Sproy

Spryflajer

Ungler Water Mungler

Bletchling

So now you know what the Bletchling looks like.
Imagine a hundred million of them swarming over the
land like a massive buzzing death cloud. Next time I'll
tell you when they're coming and what to do . . .

. . . there's nothing you can do.